WHO DO YOU SEE?

THE STRUGGLES OF
AN AFRICAN AMERICAN TEENAGE BOY

CREATED BY SEAN GEORGE, M.ED., MBA
ILLUSTRATED BY CAMERON WILSON

Sean George Enterprises
3330 Cobb Parkway
Suite 324-251
Acworth, GA. 30101

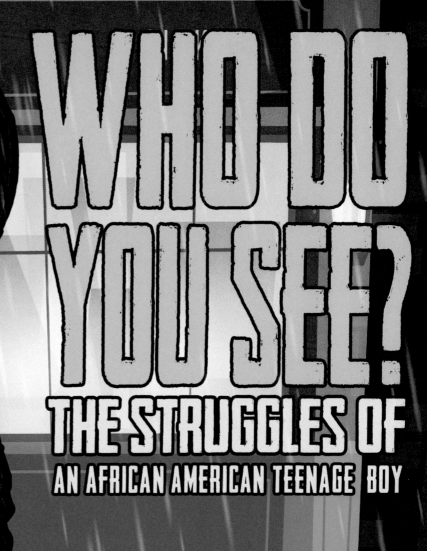

African American teenage boys are the victims of stereotypes and misconceptions on a daily basis. This is one teen's story.

For my wife Maritza and children: Shawn, Amanda, Sanaa and Nicole.

-Sean

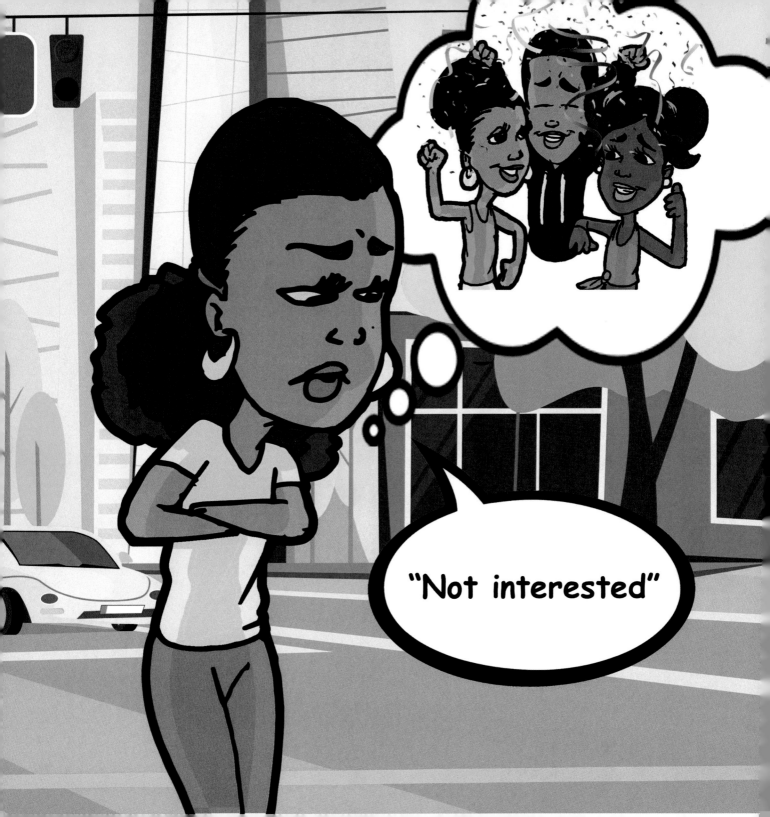

ABOUT THE AUTHOR

SEAN GEORGE has been in education for 20 years; he holds teaching certificates in Mathematics, English/Language Arts, and Social Sciences; and he is the Founder/CEO of Ties That Make A Difference, Inc., a 501©3 nonprofit organization. Ties That Make A Difference, Inc. is a 501©3 nonprofit whose mission is: To tie together faith, family, and community in order to help all youth and young adults, especially those who are considered at-risk, to excel academically, make a difference in the world by blessing others, and discover and pursue their dreams and career goals using the Bible as the foundation. He also holds a Bachelor's of Arts (BA) degree in Mass Communications/ Public Relations from Morehouse College, a Master's of Education/Mathematics (M.Ed.) degree from Cambridge College, and a Master's in Business Administration (MBA)/ Project Management degree from Walden University.

SEAN GEORGE is no stranger to stereotypes and misconceptions. He is an African American male from the inner city of Boston, who stutters, and who was part of the first group of students who could attend desegregated schools in Massachusetts. It is his belief that awareness and healthy dialogue are the beginnings to combatting stereotypes and misconceptions.

SEAN GEORGE lives with his wife Maritza and daughter Sanaa in Georgia. He also has three grown children: Shawn and Amanda, and a new daughter, Nicole, who is married to his son Shawn.

COMING SOON!

"WHO DO YOU SEE?"
SERIES BOOK 2

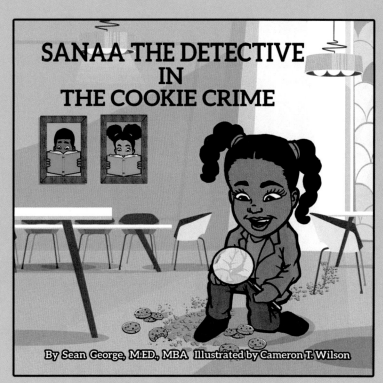

"SANAA THE DETECTIVE"
SERIES BOOK 1

Made in United States
Orlando, FL
14 June 2023

34134604R00018